ARE WE THERE YET?

A STORY BY **DAN SANTAT**

ANDERSEN PRESS

The car trip to visit Grandma is always exciting!

But after the first hour,

it can feel like an eternity.

You might find yourself saying things like,

or,

Staring out your window at a thousand miles of road can get boring pretty quickly. Not even all the toys in the world can help.

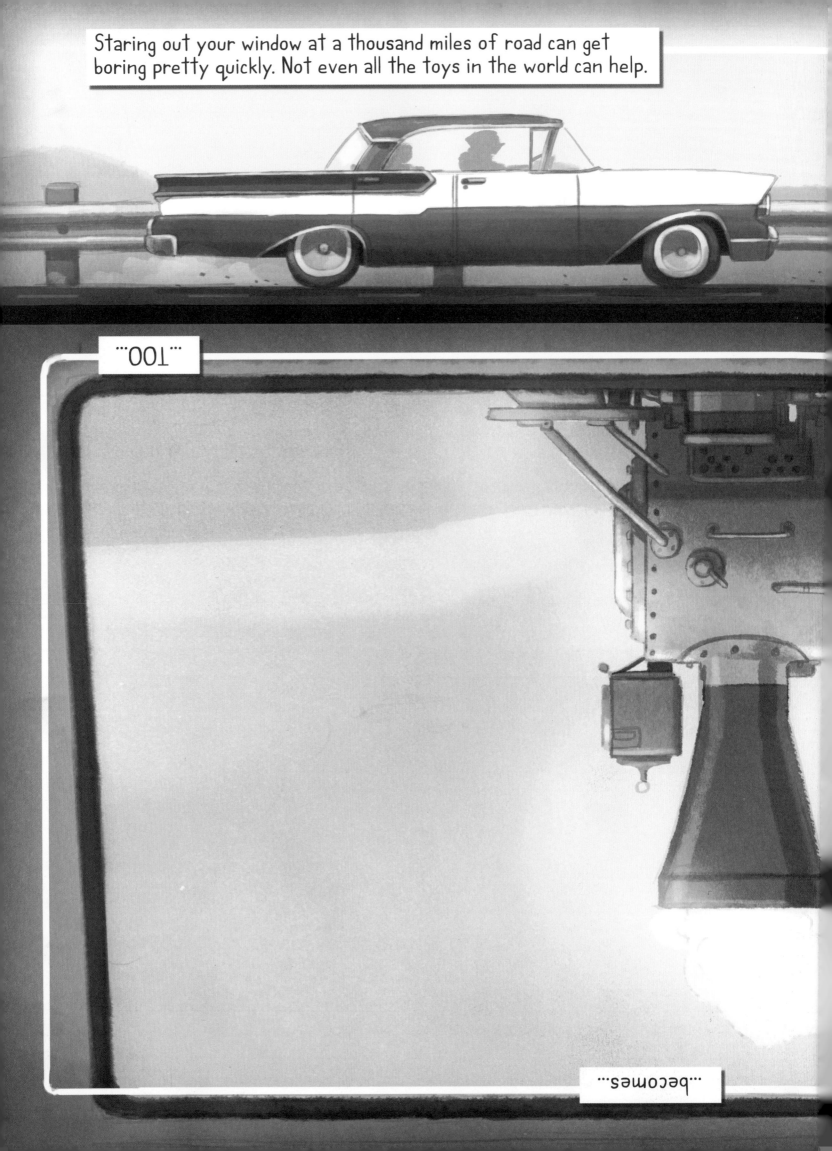

...TOO...

...becomes...

Minutes begin to feel like hours.

"This will just be a quick trip," your parents promised...
I have to go to the bathroom.
2BZK131

...but it feels like it's been a million years.

Maybe it will fly by too quickly.

257 Caplan Avenue?

That's Grandma's address.

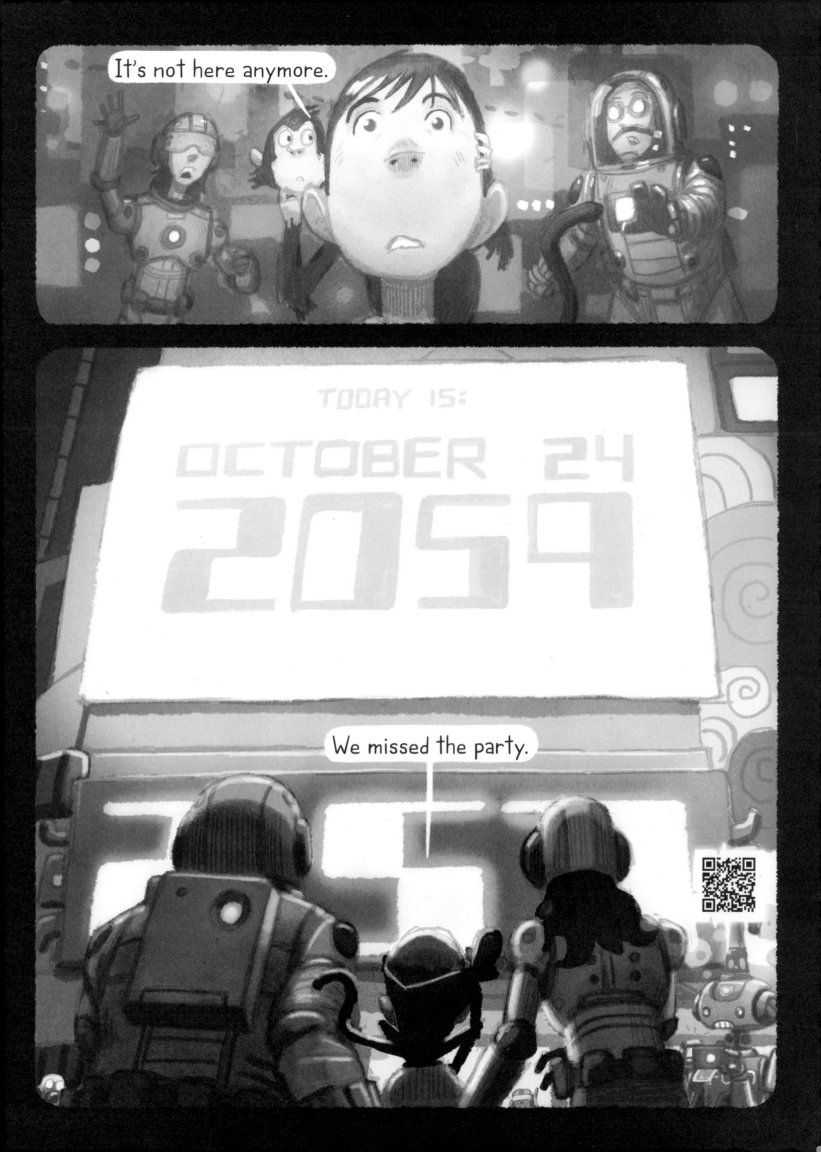

The road is full of twists and turns...

And you... ...never... ...know...

 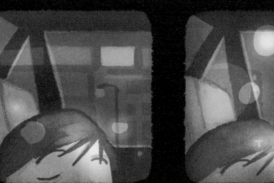 

...where... ...life... ...may...

...take... ...you.

So sit back and enjoy the ride.

But remember, there's no greater gift than the present.

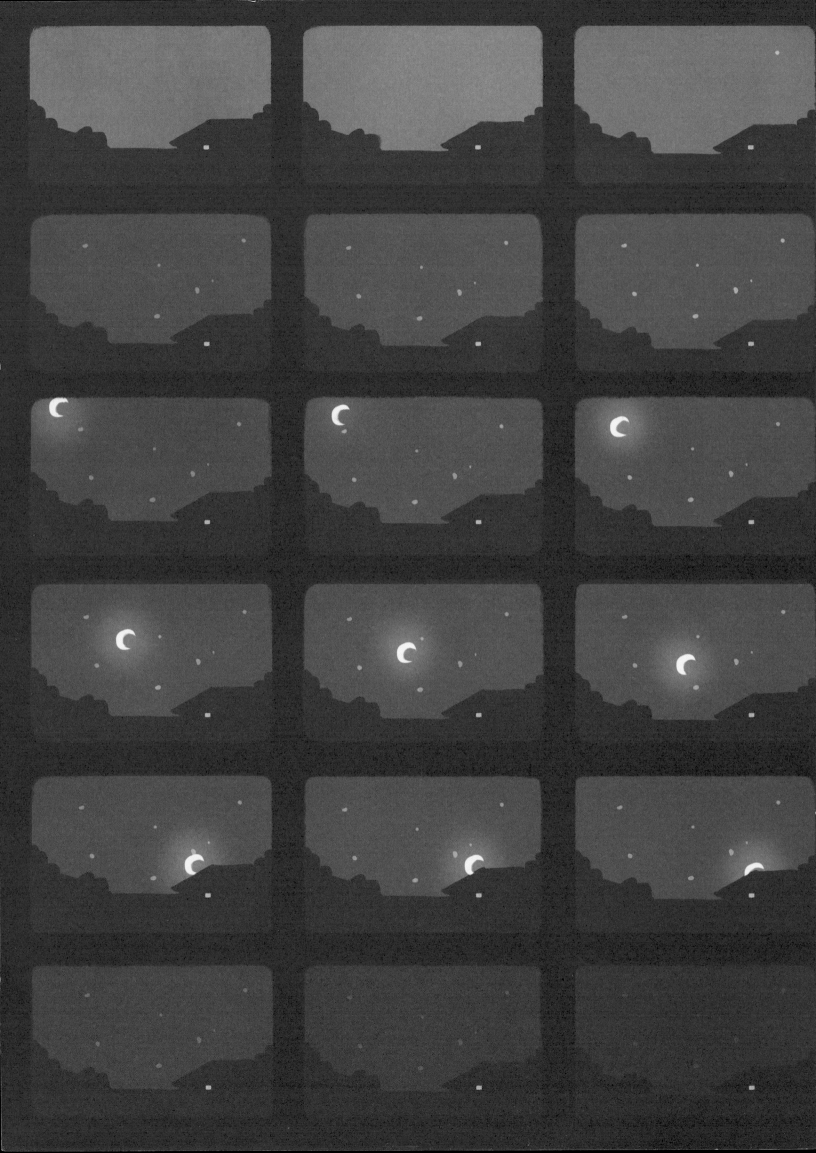